DREGS

DREGS

Rachel K Jones

Rainy Arvo Press

Contents

Dedication	vii
The Viking Poem	1
The Pitch	3
The Pocket Conundrum	13
The Tree	24
Jim builds a chariot	27
Leave not a piece of me behind	39
One More No More	41
Selling Lies	47
Effie's Eye	59
101 Words	62
Rainy Day - Easy Prey.	63
Poetry Snacks	67
Cenotaph	68
The Slips	71

The Unbearable Weight of Truth	76
Her Solitude	79
Crossing on a burnt bridge	85
Chairs to be stacked away, please.	89
A note from the author.	95
Made Away Themselves	97
Prologue	99
Chapter One	101
Contact Me	107
About The Author	108
Useful Stuff	109
Notes	110

Dedication and Thanks

Steve Jones: My love, my life, my everything.
I am blaming you for all of this. Thank you for believing in me.

Alison Supernak: I told you I would dedicate a book to you. I miss you. EAD.

Angela and The Pubsters: Thanks for your unending support.
I could have never started on this journey without you.

Dad: I wish you could have been around to read this. You introduced me to the interesting and the absurd. Thank you.

My little gang of beta-readers: Duffy, Henry, Chiara, Jaymee and Taffy. Love you guys.

My gratitude goes to all of you that have kept me going, inspired me to be better, and cared for me during hard times.
You know who you are. Thank you.

Copyright © 2022 by Rachel K Jones

All rights reserved. No part of this book may be reproduced in any manner whatsoever without written permission except in the case of brief quotations embodied in critical articles and reviews.

First Printing, April 2022

The Viking Poem

Oh! To be a Viking,
And sail the seven seas.
With horns stuck on your helmet
And currant buns for tea.

Oh! To have a beard
That reaches to your feet.
And don't forget, it's a safety-net
For anything you eat.

by Rachel Burgess (age 9)

The Pitch

Once again, Alex had deployed her emergency handbag knickers. If a bus mowed her down, at least her mother would be proud of her daughter's clean underwear. She was late. She was later than late. The likelihood of her being killed by rush hour traffic was high, considering the way she dashed across the busy roads.

Even though her clean undergarments provided some comfort, she felt as rough as a puking cat. What had she been drinking? Oh God, Southern Comfort? Her guts roiled at the memory. Standing on the kerb, she leant forward, depositing her breakfast into a fast-food container. Cracking shot, Alex. You might still salvage this day after all. It was a relief this happened before she got to the office.

"It is your own fault, idiot," she said aloud, provoking a glare from a fellow pedestrian. "No, not you!" she called after the retreating suit. "Me!"

Clearing her throat into the gutter a final time, she ruefully eyed the bilious mess resembling, to her disgust, something like a fur ball. She couldn't go into the meeting with breath like a twelve-year-old tabby. This demanded coffee and air freshener.

A hole-in-the-wall coffee kiosk beckoned from across the road, and she ducked through the traffic, tempting death or worse. Inside, a young man sat staring into the middle distance, apparently not noticing when Alex stepped forward. She waved her hand in front of his face, and he blinked, slowly, with an almost reptilian languor. Spotting her, he smiled, nodded, and pointed to the chalkboard menu.

The choices were few, but Alex didn't care; she needed strong, dark coffee, the sort that didn't mess about. Coffee with both attitude and flavour. Turning to order, she found the guy staring into space again. Was he stoned? She leaned into the serving hatch, breathing in dark-brown fragrances that promised so much. She smiled.

Cluttered around the counter was a haphazard collection of sundries for sale, extending on past the shiny espresso machine. Not all boxes appeared labelled in English, cheap knockoffs, probably. Then, in the gloom, she spotted a box of toothbrushes. Perfect. Today was going to be a success, she thought. The Universe is aligning itself for me.

"Hi!" she sang out to the reluctant barista, "A double espresso and a toothbrush, please?"

"Double espresso and two cups?" he replied.

"No, a double espresso and a toothbrush," repeated Alex in a louder voice. She pointed over his shoulder to what she wanted.

He peered into the back, spotted the box, and his eyes lit up with understanding. He laughed, "Yes, of course!", and retrieved the box, standing it on the counter for Alex to browse.

As he busied himself with the clatter of cups and hissing coffee apparatus, Alex selected a pink toothbrush. "Excuse me," she asked. "Do you sell toothpaste?"

He turned and shrugged. "Not sure. I'll have a check in a minute, after I finish your coffee."

"Thanks."

Soon, Alex's coffee appeared through the hatch, wisps of steam escaping from the plastic lid. The young man disappeared into the dark, and Alex heard boxes bumping around. After a few seconds, he reappeared with a striped white and turquoise tube. "I think this is it," he said. "It's in Chinese or something, so I don't know what flavour it is."

"All good. Thanks," said Alex, pleased to find what she needed so quickly. She paid, gulped down her coffee, and left the empty cup behind. Now her motor was up and running, and all she needed was to sneak into the toilets, quickly freshen up, and she would be ready to go.

Today was an important day. It was her first company pitch meeting, and a strong impression would go a long way. Hopefully Chloe, her manager, would not be in the session. This was Alex's day to shine, and she did not want to be subjected to the harridan's constant criticism.

Chloe's team consisted of overblown, hee-haw types. Their joint projects grew legs, although some had a noticeable limp. There were no tangible outcomes that she had ever seen. Alex felt that not only did the emperor have no clothes, but he had an arrow pointing towards his genitalia.

Ahead of her, office blocks reared into the sky, the one she was headed for plainly visible. Checking her watch, Alex silently cursed before picking up speed.

***

She arrived on the tenth floor with little fuss and ducked into the restroom. At the sink, she quickly tamed her ratty hair with a vicious brushing before retrieving the toothbrush and brightly coloured tube from the bottom of her bag. Fearing she was about to smear haemorrhoid ointment inside her mouth, she tried deciphering the foreign text. Only two words of English jumped out at her, "Preppermine Troothpaste". Oh well, she thought, at least it doesn't say "Bum Bum Cream".

Eager to be moving, she scrubbed last night's debauchery away with a flourish of fluoride. It tasted minty and sharp, as Alex brushed her tongue, trying not to gag as she did. Checking her reflection, she bared her teeth in the mirror, marvelling at the almost Hollywood perfection.

Great teeth, rotten hangover. It was a shame she couldn't do anything for her pounding head. It felt as though it would pop her eyes out of her skull.

Pushing her headache away, she tried to ignore the growing pressure. She hoped she could struggle through the next hour without having a stroke. "Don't be so dramatic!" she told the young woman in the mirror.

***

In the corridor, Alex spotted Brian from Purchasing slinking towards her. He was a sleaze-ball of the lowest order, a middle-aged cephalopod with an enlarged prostate, and she always avoided him at work functions. She shuddered, relieved when he sidestepped into his office to answer a persistent phone.

"Dirty pervert!" she yelled down the hall. Shocked by her outburst, she clamped a hand over her mouth. This was going to be one hell of a hangover to ride out, apparently, and she needed to toughen up. Perhaps the coffee was a bad idea.

Too late now. It was eight-thirty already, and the meeting was about to start. Noticing the boardroom door ajar, Alex slipped in, relieved no one spotted her as she took a seat towards the middle of the oval table. Not too presumptuous, but not too restrained either. Score one for me, she thought.

Felicity, Alex's assistant, placed a coffee and biscuit before her with a smile and a wink. "I saw you sneaking in," she said. "Drink it while it's hot."

"Thanks, Flick," said Alex. "You're too talented for this place. This lot don't appreciate you."

Felicity blushed, smiled weakly, and glanced away. The rest of the room stared at Alex, their eyebrows raised in mild consternation.

"That was a bit loud," whispered Felicity. "Thanks all the same, though." She squeezed Alex's arm as she walked away.

"Time to begin, I think," boomed the distinctive voice of Nick Westall, Head of Commercial Accounts. The room quietened as people sat, shuffled their papers, and pulled pens from pockets. With a sense of approaching disaster, Alex realised she was sitting directly opposite Chloe. The older woman's mouth was crinkled by years of smoking, and frown lines furrowed her sallow skin, turning her face into some kind of relief map. *Like Nosferatu's less attractive sister*, mused Alex, causing an escaped giggle to quickly be turned into a cough. *Get a grip on yourself*, she thought.

"Ladies and Gentlemen, may I introduce Paul Kramer from BioFutures," continued Nick, nodding to a casually dressed man on his left. "Paul is here to discover what ClearView can offer as both a media creative, and client focused, service. I know you will give him your full attention."

He motioned to Paul, who smiled around the room. "Hi," he said. "I hear ClearView is the best of the best, so I am here for some inspiration and help with planning. I'm sure most of you have read our company vision document, but I'll give you a quick recap anyway."

A gentle chuckle went round the table at that.

"They'll need it," Alex muttered under her breath, before quickly tapping her pen against her teeth, the picture of innocence. Not everyone appeared to have heard her, thankfully. Only Chloe held her gaze from across the table, her cryogenic stare causing Alex to swallow any further comments.

Paul carried on, as promised, "BioFutures is an ethically driven development company, dedicated to creating positive impacts in emerging economies. We are working towards a healthier, inclusive future for upcoming generations. Making a big difference through small projects."

Murmurs of approval echoed around the table. A man leant forward, clearing his throat. "Paul," he said. "I'm James Carver, creative team lead. First, let me say how thrilled we are to have you on board."

Alex snorted. Loudly.

With a filthy look in her direction, James continued. "Our best minds have been on your wish list for weeks, dedicating themselves to ensuring you, as our client, receive a quality package."

Alex snorted again. *Come on*, she told herself. Pretending to cough, she said, "Allergies, sorry!"

Now it was Chloe's turn to speak, "Chloe Monthall, project liaison. Firstly, Paul, may I say how pleased we are to be part of such a forward-thinking initiative. ClearView has always prided itself on its commitment to a sustainable future."

"Ha! Bollocks!" shouted Alex, hurriedly pushing her fist into her mouth to stop the tirade threatening to escape.

The whole boardroom stared at her, expressions filled with murderous hatred.

Chloe ignored Alex, soldiering on. "We thought we should start with a balloon launch from the White Cliffs of Dover. Ten-thousand helium balloons, displaying your logo, released over the sea to signify your global reach."

Paul's eyes widened. "Oh, well, that sounds, erm..." he stuttered.

James took over the pitch. "After the balloons, we thought we might distribute a few thousand crates of hi-energy drinks to some of the migrant camps, again, all with your logo. Showing how you encourage people to keep striving. After which, we will send a dozen inflatable goalposts to a warzone of your choice. With footballs, of course, all sporting your brand. Because BioFutures is all about kicking goals."

Paul, appearing pale in the tenth-floor windows' light, blinked once. Then he blinked again.

"You are fucking idiots!" yelled Alex, on her feet now. "You are the most tone-deaf bunch of prats I've ever met." She was conscious she may well be washing her job down the river; the debris of her career and reputation floating like logs in the torrent, but she didn't care. "What the hell kind of half-arsed, misbegotten campaign is this?"

"Sit down, Alex!" snapped Chloe. "I apologise, Paul, this is her first pitch meeting."

"No, I won't sit down, you dried up hag. Don't think I haven't seen you, with your crafty morning vodka shot and choc-chip muffin. You're defunct, love. Your kind of strategies went out with shiny disco pants. As a matter of fact, I hear you were a bit of a dancefloor-whore in your day, Chloe. Also, we all know it was you who gave Brian the clap. Guess what? He then gave it to Syriana in HR."

Everything tumbled out of her now, three years of nodding and pretending everything was fine. The dam had burst, and she was unable to stop the flood of words rushing from her.

"This man needs an agency who understands what he does. His plans won't come to fruition this year or even next. He is investing in the future! You lot want to pollute the English Channel, give migrants diabetes, and play football with traumatised kids. You want to stamp his company name all over that mess? Who do you think you are? Inflatable goal posts? Seriously?"

Alex stopped, needing to breathe for a beat before continuing. "Don't you dare reach for the phone, Nick, or I'll let everyone know your nasty little secrets." She looked around the table. "Ask him why his wife left him. Go on, ask him. Came home and found him in a compromising position wearing a beagle costume, didn't she? Grubby little man. I'm surprised he manages to make it to work without chasing the mailman, and peeing on every lamppost on the way in."

People began pushing their chairs away from the table as she locked gazes with each in turn, condemnations uttered with every word. "Embezzler. Alcoholic. Narcissist. Philanderer. Plagiarist. Not you, Felicity, you're lovely. Abuser. Drunk-driver. Do I need to go on?"

The room was now a tableau, people frozen to the spot. Only Felicity moved, staring at her colleagues, horrified.

"I'm sorry, Paul, that you came to this pathetic colony of maggots for help. I'm sorry they couldn't see you are working to better everyone's tomorrow. I'm especially sorry that no one, not one single person, researched you properly. I did, and I am deeply moved by your vision. I hope you eventually do find some quality representation. You deserve better than these idiots."

"Alex Cochrane, you're fired!" screamed Nick. "Collect your belongings and get out!"

"Woof!" barked Alex. "Fuck off, Snoopy!" She was flagging now, the flood subsiding as she ran out of words.

"Alex Cochrane, will you come work for BioFutures now that you are freelance?" asked Paul. "I promise, all I'm into is drunken karaoke."

"Why me?" enquired a now exhausted Alex.

"Because I have been doing this long enough to recognise passion and authenticity. You possess both, and I want you on my team."

"Actually, I think I may be slightly over-caffeinated. I don't normally go off like that."

"Oh, I'm a caffeine head too, Alex, we'll get on well. What do you say?"

Alex nodded. "Let's do it! I'm always up for an adventure."

Gathering her stuff together from where it was strewn across the floor during her outburst, she came across the stripy white tube. Examining it closely, she realised it was clearly labelled "Peppermint Truthpaste", and she laughed aloud. How extraordinary.

On the way out of the room with her new boss, she gave Chloe the finger, just as Felicity slipped past. Her assistant had a box in one hand as she headed for her desk, her intentions plain. Well done, Flick, thought Alex.

Emergency knickers still in situ, the former employee of ClearView reflected that it had turned out to be a very good day indeed.

The Pocket Conundrum

Mark read the leaflet again, hoping to glean some further information. It was an innocuous trifold of glossy paper. A single word appeared, "Welcome". The rest of the paper, front and back, was blank.

He folded the paper into a small square, then felt for his front pocket. He missed the pocket's opening on the first pass and ran his hand back over his thigh to find it. Looking down, he frowned as he realised that his pocket was gone. His jeans looked the same as they ever did. He could see where the yellowed stitching was, but the fabric was smooth. He looked at his left side, feeling once again for a pocket. The half-moon curve of the motif was clear, but he could access no pocket. He grabbed behind him, feeling his own rear. The denim was flat; he felt no ridges or stitching.

He dropped the paper, moving his hands up his body. It felt normal. He put his arms out in front of him, turning his palms over to inspect them.

Bending down, he examined his shoes. They were his

favourite brown brogues. Something was off about the laces, though. Instead of laying in neat beige bows, they both appeared as a Mobius strip. There was no beginning or end to them.

He straightened himself, frowning and narrowing his eyes. Nothing was making any sense.

"What the hell is going on?" he mumbled.

"Hey! New Boy!" A shout came from somewhere off to his right.

"Coo-ee! Over here!"

Mark turned to face the voice. His head swam with the sudden movement. He felt decidedly queasy.

"Hey! Don't you dare throw up; we haven't got time." said a large, ruddy faced man folded behind the wheel of a golf buggy. He got out, extricating his huge frame with considerable effort. He loomed towards Mark, holding out a hand the size of a shovel.

"I'm Griff. Nice to meet you." said Griff.

Mark politely returned the handshake.

"I'm Mark. I think." he replied.

"Course you are, New Boy. Whatever you say." said Griff.

"I'm not really sure where I am," said Mark. He looked up at Griff, hoping for some answers.

"Yep, you're a New Boy, alright!" laughed Griff. "Come on, get in, Champ. I'll take you to the Review Centre."

Griff began the process of shoe-horning his own enormous form into the golf buggy. Mark watched his efforts for a while before helping him get the last of his buttocks into the seat.

"Cheers, pal," said Griff. He was puffing hard to regain his breath. "Hop in, then. I ain't got all day."

Mark squeezed himself into the other seat, wedging himself against the low side of the vehicle in case Griff expanded his bulk any further. For a moment, Mark didn't think that the buggy would move with all the weight it carried. The electric motor whirred and revved, then finally spun the wheels so that they were travelling. As they motored on, Mark studied his surroundings. Whilst he had been wondering about his pockets, he had been totally unaware of his location. Things were now coming into view. It was as though his long-distance focus was working again.

They were driving along a broad city street. The buildings themselves looked ordinary. Interspersed with the retail and service premises were cafes and cake shops. There was a large frontage which read "Sisyphus Roller Bowl" in art deco style neon. The foyer was full of people standing in line.

"What's that place? " Mark asked his companion.

"Sissy's Rink? That's been there forever. Roller skating, for the damned." He chuckled, jiggling the cart as they moved along.

"What do you mean?"

"Well, Sissy's is a place where once you skate, you can't stop."

"Is it very popular then? I saw people waiting."

"Newbie, do yourself a favour. Don't go to Sissy's. Not unless you want to be skating uphill forever. It's a bad place in a bad place. If you catch my drift."

They passed a handful of eateries and bars. Some stood

out more than others because of the crowds outside. Mark watched as the small group of people waiting by the "Big Table Long Spoons" reluctantly entered the premises.

Driving by the ear-splitting screeching that howled its way out of the open door of "The Feedback Bar", Griff winced and looked at Mark. "I hate that place," he said. "Don't go there, neither."

The commercial premises soon gave way to a more residential area. Elegant houses sat behind neatly clipped lawns. In some front yards, people were gardening, weeding, or otherwise busy. Young children whizzed around on brightly coloured bikes, whilst teens lounged on front porches reading. Everything was picture perfect. Brochure families living a QR code life under an excruciatingly blue sky. Mark shook his head to clear the fuzziness.

Something was wrong. He felt his heart writhing in his ribcage, trying to escape.

Something was wrong here. Except here wasn't here.

"There it is," said Griff, as he brought the buggy to a stop at the bottom of some steps. The Review Centre."

Mark looked at the steps. They led to a large, sandy coloured building. It appeared to be all walls and no windows. The sign read "Welcome".

"Out you get, Newbie. Time to get started."

"Where do I go?" asked Mark.

"Well, I reckon that arrow which says, 'This Way' might be a good start."

Mark spotted the arrow and started towards it.

"Hey, New Boy! Don't forget your luggage." Griff gestured at the back of the buggy.

"What luggage?" said Mark. He saw a black holdall in the rear seats. "That's not mine!"

"Yes, it is, Newbie. You are now responsible for that bag and all its contents. Now get it off my buggy. I got another pickup in twenty."

Mark reached in and pulled the bag towards him, lifting it away from the vehicle. It wasn't heavy, but it was bulky and awkward. Griff honked the horn and pulled away from Mark, leaving him standing with his unfamiliar luggage.

He lifted the bag to his shoulder and followed the sign, which pointed up the steps towards the giant sandcastle. At least now he had one piece of solid information with which to work. The arrow giving him a clear direction. At the top of the stairs, he found himself faced with a huge doorway. The left side of the double doors was open, and a line of people stood in front of it, waiting. He found his way to the back of the line and stood there. In front of him, a young woman was having difficulties with her holdall. She and Mark had identical bags. Mark glanced down the line. Everybody had the same bag.

"Bit weird, innit?" someone said behind him.

Mark turned to see a young man who had a moustache that looked weeks old but was as thin as a lawyer's promise. His face had not been grown into yet, his ears on loan from an elderly bus driver.

"What?" said Mark.

"Weird, innit? All this lot. All lining up like they're going to see the Queen." He hopped from one foot to the other, glancing about constantly.

"Actually, mate, I have no idea what is going on," said Mark. "I've been sent up here. This isn't even my bloody bag."

"Ha ha ha! Good one. I'll believe ya. Thousands wouldn't!" scoffed the youth. The bouncing continued.

"Come on then, smart arse. What is all this?"

"Don't get your knickers in a twist, mate." He stopped bouncing and looked at Mark with a new focus. "You don't know, do ya? You got no idea, have ya?"

"About what?" Mark said. He could feel his irritation rising. "What don't I know? Who the fuck are you anyway, you little shit?"

"Oi! Oi! Grandad! Don't carry on like that. I'm Titus, which is the stupidest name ever, so you can call me Tits or Scrag. Your choice." He snapped a grubby handed salute.

"Don't call me Grandad, Titus." said Mark with a grin. "I'm Mark."

"Scrag will do then, Mark. No harm done, eh?"

"No. It's all good," said Mark. "Now tell me where the hell are we and what the fuck are we waiting for?"

"Shit, this is your first time, innit?"

"First time for what?"

"Shit, mate, you had better listen to me and keep your voice down," Scrag said. He stooped a little lower, so that Mark had to bend to hear what he was whispering.

"First off, is that the bag you arrived with?"

"Yes,' Mark replied.

"Well, that's one thing, at least. Do not swap or lend or let that bloody thing out of your sight. You get me?"

"Okay."

"See how that bag has no zips or catches or anything?"

Mark examined his bag. It was smooth and there seemed to be no way to access the contents. "Yes," he replied.

"That's so nothing gets in or out. Yours is yours. Mines is mines." He pointed to his own bag. It looked much heavier than Mark's.

"What's in the bags?" asked Mark.

"Everything, mate. Every little word, gesture, omission, deed, or thought that you have ever had or done in your life. Which, by the way, you don't live in anymore."

Mark shook his head. "What? I don't get it. What do you mean?"

"You're brown bread, mate. Dead. As a fucking dodo."

"No, I'm not. I'm standing here in a queue waiting for, waiting for..."

"Waiting for what, mate? A bloody bus? Two'll come along at once, you'll see!" Scrag laughed. It was not a comforting sound.

The woman in front of them shuffled forward in the line. Her bag was heavy, and she struggled to lift it. Mark leant forward to help. Scrag dragged him backwards by the collar.

"Are you a fucking idiot? What did I just tell you about these bloody bags?"

"I was only trying to help," Mark whispered.

"If you touch that bag, you keep it forever. Well, at least until you get inside, anyway."

The woman scowled at Mark and effortlessly hefted her bag onto her shoulder, striding forward to her place in line.

"See?" said Scrag. "Silly cow, thinks it's my first time, too." He gave her the finger.

"Scrag, enough about the bags. What do you mean every thought, deed, erm, whatever, action stuff?"

"Mate. Mark. Mr Blobby whoever you are, now you aren't. This is the Hall of Judgement. You are here because you died. Died somehow. Hope you were hang-gliding naked over Stonehenge or something good when you popped your clogs."

"Died?" Mark sank to his haunches. He couldn't make any sense of it at all. He should be drinking coffee on the waterfront. He was drinking coffee down at The Boathouse. They did a fantastic breakfast on a Sunday. His favourite place for the weekend, followed by a stroll along the sand to the other end of the bay. That was what he was doing.

He turned to Scrag. "I'm supposed to be having my Sunday coffee."

"Sorry mate, you're here now. I know it's a shock, 'specially the first time."

"Where are we, though? If I'm dead, why aren't I floating around on a cloud or in a fiery pit?"

Scrag chuckled, "You Newbies are hilarious. You don't get clouds or coals until you get through this bit. If you're lucky, you'll get the ole' catapult and 'Boing!' you're out of here."

The line shuffled forward again. They were nearly at the door. Mark felt the fear build in his belly. He could now see what was inside the building. Something like airport security checkpoints stood in front of them. Each person walked forward, put their bag on the conveyor belt, and stepped through the metal detector. On top of the covered belt, there were half a dozen lights. Mark could not see what was happening on the other side of the barriers. He had a feeling of dread that slowly crawled from his throat into his mouth.

The woman was at her checkpoint now. She threw her bag onto the moving belt, snarled at the agent, and walked through the detector. Every light, alarm, buzzer, and beeper went off around her. The cacophony was unbearable. Both Mark and Scrag covered their ears.

"Oh-ho!" laughed Scrag. "Bet you're glad you didn't have her bag, eh?"

Mark watched as a dozen uniformed guards ran into the screening area to drag her away as she spat and writhed under their brutal handling. What kind of place was this?

"Next please," said the agent at the gate.

Mark felt Scrag's hand on his arm. "You'll be fine, mate. I've got a good feeling about you. See you around," he said.

"Thanks, Scrag. Good luck to you, too."

Mark stepped forward and placed his bag on the belt, it wasn't very heavy, and he felt silly putting a nearly empty bag through the machine. He walked through the scanner towards the agent on the other side.

Suddenly, the lights and sirens began again. Mark covered his head with his arms, waiting for the blows to arrive. This was it. The first day of the rest of his afterlife and he was fucked already.

Still cowering, he risked opening one eye. He spotted Scrag and his crazy ears laughing and pointing at him across the concourse.

"I told ya, Mark. I told ya I had a good feeling. It's the catapult for you, boy!"

"What? What's the catapult? Scrag, what's the catapult?"

Scrag disappeared into the distance as if someone had sucked him into the background. Around him, the alarms shrieked, and his ribs crashed against his heart. Shit, that hurt and kept hurting.

Shut those fucking alarms off, he thought. That shrieking, squawking racket. Fucking seagulls. Where did the bloody seagulls come from?

He opened his eyes. A crowd of people stared down at him, a pair of hands was rhythmically pumping on his chest. He coughed. He gurgled.

"Jesus!" said Mark. "Stop it, will you?" He sat up, confused to see that he was sitting on the sand.

A woman knelt beside him and hugged him to her, kissing his cheek. "Thank you. Thank you," she repeated over and over.

Behind her, on the seafront, a boy was being examined by a paramedic. He sat on the rear step of the ambulance, wrapped in a silver blanket.

Mark felt a hefty hand on his shoulder. He gazed up into the ruddy face of another paramedic.

"Come on, Champ. Let's get you to the hospital for a check over," he said. "It's not every day you save a kid's life and nearly drown yerself."

"What?" said Mark. "What?"

He felt himself being lifted on to a stretcher. He watched the beach from his horizontal position as they carried him up towards the roadway. Drawing level with the ambulance, the boy turned towards him, emerging from the blanket. His unfortunate ears sprang out on either side of his head.

He grinned at Mark. Jumping down from the ambulance, he ran over to him.

"Thanks, Grandad," he said. "Told you I had a good feeling about you."

The Tree

    Behind our houses stands a tree
A solitary guard of green
At night it sings its songs to me
By day it casts a dappled sheen.

    "Hack it down!" I heard them cry
"It blocks the sun at noon of day
And soon the summer will pass by
Let the kids have light to play."

    I told them that this tree did more
Than stop them having summer fun
It shelters them from what's in store
When all the other seasons come.

    But they didn't hear above the sound
Of their most efficient lumber saws
And as my tree fell to the ground
I swear I heard a woody roar.

Now in the sun they sit and fry
Under parasols that block the light
With their hands they shield their eyes
Watering brown lawns every night.

In winter they are quite surprised
That rain can really fall *that* hard
As clothes whip from their washing lines
And snow just drifts across their yards.

And as for me, I draw my blinds
It aches my heart to look and see
The empty space that just reminds
Behind our houses stood a tree.

Jim builds a chariot

Sunday-January 10th, 2021. 10am

Dobbs scratched his chins. All of them. He shook his head and peered more closely at Jim.

His eyebrows knitted together, forming a horizontal question mark.

"Are you sure about this, mate?" he said.

"Bloody right, I am," said Jim. "Been thinking about it for a little while."

"It's a bit grim though, don't ya think?"

"Nah, not really. This way, I have a bit of a say and I save a wedge of cash, too."

Dobbs exhaled through flabby lips, horse-like. His face in motion, flitting between bewilderment and inspiration.

"Okay," he said, finally.

Jim nodded and reached across to shake his friend's hand.

"That's the go, Dobbsy!" He gave Dobbs a mile-wide grin.

"Right," said Dobbs. "I'll grab the gear out of the Ute. May as well crack on."

"Not yet, mate, first let me show you the tree," said Jim. *"Then you'll see what I mean."*

Wednesday-March 17th, 2021. 7pm

Jim ran his hand over the smooth wood. Dobbs had done a bloody good job. The grain had come alive in his talented hands. The sunset's glow gave the red gum's veins a vitality even within its current mawkish setting.

Jim chuckled to himself as he realised that the felled and finished eucalypt held more life in it than he did. He remembered reading that the River Red Gum may live for well over a hundred years. Jim understood that his remaining days numbered far fewer than that.

He stroked the wooden surface, enjoying the familiar scent of eucalyptus, letting memories tumble across his mind.

It was time.

He needed to convince Andrea to stop fussing for five minutes and start making plans. There were phone calls to make.

He locked up the shed and headed towards the house; the sun setting behind him as he stepped onto the veranda. There was still enough daylight to make out the small stairway, but it was fading away rapidly, succumbing to the violet dusk.

Thursday-June 24th, 2021. 11am

Brayden stuck his tongue out to one side, a pink blob of concentration. He held his paintbrush tightly in his fist. His strokes delicately placed.

He managed to make shapes and not mess. He squished one final purple lump into his masterpiece, stepped back, and smiled.

"I did it, Poppy!" he said, looking at Jim. "I made you the carry thing!"

Jim leant forward to examine the four-year-old's efforts. He saw a definite shape to the picture, some wheels, and a figure with almost the right number of limbs for a human.

Jim chuckled, gathering his grandson into his arms, perching him on his knee.

"It's wonderful, Brayden. Poppy's chariot!" he said. He pointed to another smaller shape in the painting.

"What's this one?" he said.

"My truck," said the boy. "I'm coming with you."

Jim's breath caught in his throat. He squeezed the little one to him, shaking his head.

"No buddy, you can't come with me. I've got to go on this trip on my own."

"Poppy, I want to co— "

"Brayden, mate, I have to head off alone. One day when you are older, you'll understand why."

"Mummy says that you are sick, and you can't be not sick even with doctor medicine."

"Yes, she's right, son. Not even with doctor medicine."

Brayden shifted on Jim's lap, his brown eyes studying his grandpa's face. He reached up and kissed Jim on the cheek.

"Love you, Poppy," he said. "Can I paint more trucks?"

"Just one more truck," said Jim. "We've got to leave some space for all the other bludgers!"

"Bludgers!" said Brayden and turned back to his palette.

Monday-September 20th, 2021. 12pm

This was a thing of beauty, a marvel of creation, the seventeenth wonder of the world. That was how Jim described it to Dobbs.

Andrea, however, thought it a bloody nuisance and the thing impeded her housework. She was forced to arrange all the other furniture around it so that the television remained visible without anyone having to perform complicated yoga stretches.

She had to admit, though, that she enjoyed the artwork and messages of love that slowly filled the empty wooden surfaces. Most of the family had added their "Bon Voyage" wishes and little doodles over the past three or four months. It was certainly a talking point, and Andrea knew how much it meant to Jim.

He had recently started adding little decorative knick-knacks to the sides and top. He spent a few hundred dollars in Bunnings, picking up brass screws, hooks, and trimmings. Every time they left the house, he asked to be taken to the store, "just to pick up a few bits". Andrea guessed he found some calm amongst the aisles of tools and materials. He seemed at home surrounded by the towering shelving and heady hints of solvent.

The promised year would be up soon, thought Andrea. The calendar didn't have any entries after October. All the pages appeared blank. She was not sure how to prepare for nothing. How could you have a to-do list for something your future had not guaranteed?

Looking across the room, she noticed some recent additions to the artwork. She moved closer for a better look, leaning into the smooth wood. The message brief, written in permanent marker.

"You always go missing when it is your shout, you bugger. Catch ya!"

Dobbs, who had added a smiley face as a flourish, had signed below.

Andrea smiled sadly. Time to take Jim his lunch and settle in for the afternoon.

Tuesday-October 26th, 2021. 12pm

Jim stared out of the office window. From this height, he watched the rain clouds gathering over the eastern suburbs.

In the city, however, all seemed much brighter. The sun danced on the refrigeration unit on the adjacent roof, sending flashes of light skittering across the flat surface.

High noon breathed in, everything hung in the balance.

Short shadows waited, ready to pounce once the sun began its slow fall towards the West.

Doctor Pawan turned towards Jim, speaking, using a soft tone.

Jim understood he was being told something important, but he was fascinated by the teetering sun, soon to begin its downward trajectory. He remembered a sundial that had enchanted him as a boy. He spent an entire afternoon mesmerised by the slow shadow's path. He felt like that creeping shadow, the day slipping away underneath him.

Suddenly, he understood what he needed to complete his project. They could easily pick one up on the way home. It would save having to make another trip out to the shops tomorrow.

He'd mention it to Andrea when they got back into the car. She looked a bit upset, so he would have to pick his moment. The boot was big enough. He knew the bloke in the store would help him load up.

Jim became aware that the talking had stopped, and everyone turned his way. Dr Pawan reached over and offered him his hand. Jim shook it vigorously, gratefully; happy to be getting out of the cramped office.

Time to head off.

He wouldn't miss having to come to this place again. Over the years, so much bad news had been delivered to him in this tiny room that he could almost smell the oily, smashed hopes that lay in pieces on the surrounding floor.

Tuesday-October 26th, 2021. 1.30pm

"You are being unreasonable," he said. His voice loud in the tiny car.

Andrea stamped on the brakes. Jim lurched forward into his seat belt. She turned towards him, her raw, red eyes seeking some logic in his demands.

"I am not taking you there," she said. "Not today. Not now!"

She glanced into the rear-view mirror, aware of her sudden stop. She checked the reflection. No other vehicle waited behind her, no headlights dazzling through the wet afternoon. Just the rain running in slow, sullen downward stripes on the back window.

"This will be the last time, love," said Jim. He sounded tired and a little desperate. "I promise."

The wipers were pleading rhythmically, dragging themselves across the front screen in a forlorn motion. Blades moved the rain languidly, pushing water to the edges of the glass, dissipating it along the rubber seals. She stared as the arms swiped from right to left, left to right, over and over. The noisy motion continued, relentless, on the outside of the otherwise silent car.

"Alright," she said in a small voice. "Let's not hang around, though." "Thanks, love," said Jim. She heard his smile, and she responded with one of her own as she pulled back into the traffic.

Friday-November 5th, 2021. 3am

Well then, thought Jim. *The party's over, time to turn out the lights.*

He looked around the room at the figures asleep in the dim glow. These were his most precious things, his family and friends. They leant, lay, and sat in various states of unconsciousness. Mostly sleeping silently, some softly breathing. Only Dobbs was snoring, making a noise like a buffalo on payday.

It had been a bloody great night. What a send-off. The love that filled the room was tangible. He glanced over at his Andrea; smiling as she dozed. Jim hoped she dreamt of better days. He would miss her. He regretted making her so tired over the past months. Hopefully, she could bounce back soon— once he was on his way.

Pictures of the Grandkids hung on the walls everywhere he looked. He spotted Brayden's cheeky expression in one image, holding up his favourite truck and grinning at the camera. Jim remembered taking that snap. It was the day that he had tried to explain to him what was going to happen to Poppy. Somehow the explanation became lost in translation and Brayden became convinced that Poppy needed to build a chariot to go on a trip.

Jim smiled to himself, that little fella was a live spark, for sure. He always enjoyed watching him painting and planning for the chariot's departure.

Jim glanced at the clock on the wall; just after three in

the morning. He now understood what it meant to be tired through to your bones. He felt the tug of his lungs as they tried to keep the air moving inside him. The spaces in between breaths were getting longer. Jim realised he was probably down to his last half dozen.

It was time to go. So, he went.

Just like that.

Saturday-October 20th, 2021. 10am
Jim's chariot sat in the centre of the aisle. It was hardly recognisable as the piece of beautifully crafted red gum. Around the edges were slogans, drawings, sequins, ribbons, and tassels. The lid festooned with brass fixings, paintings, Plasticine and glued on dinosaurs. There were a multitude of colours, textures, and materials stuck, taped, and nailed to every available surface.

In the centre of the lid, sat a sundial. This had been Jim's most recent purchase. Made from grey-green copper with the inscription "Tempus Fugit". Jim left specific instructions for it to be set permanently in place in his backyard in view of the kitchen window.

The gathered crowd sat, smiling at each other as they understood what Jim had conveyed to his loved ones in the creation of this project. Each person present could see their own mark that they once made on the wood, whether an image or a message.

Jim's chariot carried him, like the Egyptian God Ra, across the sky. Eternally chasing the sun towards its rest, in a vessel bound together with love and gratitude.

Following behind (but not for at least seven decades) came a little boy pedalling a truck, concentrating hard and sticking his tongue out in a pink blob.

***

Sunday-January 10th, 2021. 9.45am

"Dobbsy," Jim shouted down the phone. "You'd better get over here quick-smart! I want to build a bloody coffin."

Leave not a piece of me behind

Leave not a piece of me behind
lest a mote of me dance blissfully
racing sunlight in a dusty room.

Leave not a piece of me behind
where foot once pushed on softened soil
to leave my name in earth's remembering.

Leave not a piece of me behind
for moon-doused imps to twist and shout
and shyly peep through curtains crack'd.

Leave not a piece of me behind
like the heart's fine grist, to grit and grind
with words a-whispered claiming breath.

Instead, wind up the song, full dance the circle.
and there you'll be, and there I'll find
the piece of me I left behind.

One More No More

It was late. Even by Thoth's standards, it was late. He calculated that the drink-up had run for at least two hours later than last Tuesday. This meant that Anubis must be gearing up for a long session.

Thoth knew that tomorrow would be a shit fest when Anubis (a.k.a. Andy) the jackal-headed idiot, tried to function on hardly any sleep and a brutal hangover.

Shaking his head, he dipped his beak into his drink. This is the major difference between the two of them, he thought. Andy enjoyed having a fat dog mouth to scoop alcohol into as fast as he liked. Thoth had a beak that only held about a teaspoon of booze at any one time.

Andy had wedged himself between Osiris and Set. The three exchanged verbal blows in a heated discussion. There was lots of table-banging and loud cursing. Andy, often being the voice of reason in these drunken tussles, had become accustomed to the ruckus.

Thoth strutted across the bar to see what the fuss was about.

Set, with his reputation for loving a scrap, pointed his bony finger in Osiris's face.

"Don't call me that," he said. "Never call me that!"

"Fucking aardvark," Osiris responded. "Long-nosed git."

"You're a dick-less wonder in a pointy hat!" yelled Set. He stood, knocking the table, and spilling the drinks.

Osiris jumped to his feet, his tall crown catching in the wall light behind him. He extricated himself and glared at Set. "

They made my dick out of gold, mate. You're stuck with something the ants dragged in!" he said.

Set began squaring up to his brother, his beady eyes a-fire with fury.

"Lads, lads, lads," said Andy. "We don't need to do this every time. Ozzy, your round, mate. Take your hand off your golden wand and put it into your pocket. I'll have a pint of mild, please."

Set grinned as smugly as an aardvark could, then caught Andy's stern gaze.

"As for you," said Andy. "You're up next, so don't get too comfy."

Thoth sat down at the far end of the table as Ozzy mumbled his way past, heading off to order the next round.

"Alright, T?" Andy asked.

"Yeah, but you know it's getting late, right?" replied Thoth.

Andy nodded. "Alright, T. One more then no more, okay?" He grinned a puppy-like grin. Thoth nodded and leant back in his chair.

Across the bar, Ozzy leant on the counter, chatting to Shezmu. Shez had done rather well since taking over the pub, thought Thoth. He was only a minor deity, but he'd livened things up with his peculiar brand of hospitality and blood-slaughter. If you avoided the Thursday Trivia and Sacrifice nights, it turned out to be a comfortable place to meet up for after-work drinks.

In the far corner, a group of winged entities were crowding round the jukebox, trying to come to an agreement about which track to choose. Consensus reached, buttons pressed, the familiar opening bars of "Jolene" filled the air. Dolly was popular amongst the clientele of this establishment. They regarded her as a human worthy of immortality, if not deification.

Andy said that he couldn't wait to hold her perfect heart in his hand. He believed it would be lighter than even his smallest feather. He was a die-hard fan if truth be told.

Conversely, he waited with a hungry desire to face-down that Bieber idiot. He had some very special scales for his arrival. Thoth realised that particular day would result in some creative fudging of the figures. However, as he was the only one who kept the records, it wasn't an issue.

Ozzy came back to the table with a tray; a pint for Andy, a Guinness for Set, chardonnay in a long glass for Thoth, and a scotch for himself.

"Cheers, boys," he said. "Here's to us!"

They each raised their glasses. These four had been friends for all time and would remain so until Ra stopped sailing his barque (Boat of a Million Years, to be exact) across the sky. That crusty old sun god as reliable now as he ever was. The Afterlife had been pretty good to all of them. Mortals were sometimes a pain in the proverbial arse; some of them were so demanding nowadays, but generally everything was coming up roses.

From behind the bar came the sound of a phone ringing.

Osiris looked up, guiltily. "That'll be the missus," he said. "I'm late for dinner again."

"Tell her I already left, Shez!" he shouted to the proprietor.

Shez nodded and went to answer the call.

"I don't know how she puts up with you," said Andy. "Your Isis needs a bloody medal for being married to your lazy arse."

Set laughed, "It won't be because of his one carat surprise, anyway!"

"Andy," shouted Shez. "This call's for you. Sounds official. Do you want me to take a message?"

"Yes please, mate. Work can wait 'til tomorrow." Andy took a last swig from his glass. "Speaking of which, time to head off, lads."

Thoth breathed a sigh of relief. Perhaps tomorrow wouldn't be too bad after all. At this rate, Andy would get a decent sleep tonight. They both stood. Andy put an arm round Thoth.

"C'mon babe," he said, "Let's grab a kebab on the way home."

"Only if you promise to go easy on the spicy sauce," said Thoth. "I can't take another night of your noxious emissions."

Shez rushed over to the table, his leonine face frozen in shock. He stared from one to another, seemingly speechless.

"What is it?" asked Thoth. He could sense something doom-like lurking on the immediate horizon.

"It's Ra," gulped Shez. "He's been in an accident. His boat's fucked and no one can start the bastard thing!"

The friends stared gormlessly at each other, trying to

assess the implications of the situation. The silence grew longer and deeper.

"Shit," said Set. "How the fuck is the sun going to rise in the morning?"

"Bollocks," said Ozzy. "Looks like I won't be getting home for dinner tonight,"

"What we need, boys," said Andy. "Is a plan."

Thoth, in silence, reached inside his jacket and pulled out his pen. He grabbed his notebook; writing 'Plan A' at the top of the page, he underlined it.

"What's first?" he said as they all leant towards him.

Silence, then a confident voice rang out.

"We're going to need a bigger boat," said Ozzy.

Selling Lies

The sound of urine splashing on the back of his seat alerted Mick to the situation. He angled the mirror to view Buddy's reddening face. At least the youngster had the decency to look embarrassed.

"Sorry, Boss," he said. "Got carried away."

"Idiot," Mick replied. He knew what happened next, what it meant for them—hosing down the van when they should all be getting some sleep.

He sighed in tired resignation. Ten minutes from base, and this bunch of mongrels couldn't keep it together. Jack and Alfie, both desperate to piss, struggled forwards and relieved themselves.

"Pack it up!" shouted Mick. "It stinks in here!" When he opened the windows, there was a scramble as everyone tried to breathe the fresh night air. In his side mirrors, Mick counted four men, each with their face to the wind. He turned to Jet, his old friend and squad sergeant.

"It's the little things that keep them happy, Micky-boy," said Jet. "Let's just go home."

***

The booth at the gate appeared empty. He honked twice, and a woman emerged from the back of the structure, straightening her uniform.

"Calm down, I'm coming," she called. "No need to be rude!"

"Now then, Bindi," said Jet, leaning across a stony-faced Mick. "No need for such a fuss. You know who we are."

Bindi peered at Jet, who winked at her as he settled back into his seat.

"Sorry, Sergeant, I didn't see you there."

Addressing Mick, she held out her hand. "Report and SwOBR unit, please, Corporal.".

"Conveyance Hunt Six, all members returning. Zero passengers," he replied, passing her the testing unit. It was an old model, dented and dull. Her eyebrows raised in amusement.

"Roger, CH-6 back in. No extras. SwOBR cleared and returned," she said. "You need an upgrade for this old thing, Corporal."

"I know," he said, aware he wouldn't get any new kit this year but still smiling as he took the unit back from her.

The gate arm raised, and Mick inched the vehicle forward, waiting for the light ahead to change from red to green. All clear. Time to return to the depot, wash the piss-swill out of the back, feed the lads, and then, sleep.

***

In his quarters, Mick pulled off his musty and damp socks. Balling them up, he pitched them into the laundry skip, his dirty fatigues following. Everything stank in this tiny room.

He had been with this program for three years, with no

offer of better housing. Last year, in a fit of generosity, stores distributed some new mattresses but did nothing about the rough blankets or sweat-stained pillows. *Maybe in another three years*, he thought.

It could be worse; he could live with the rest of his squad in 'The Kennels', as they called it. There they shared dormitories and toilets, everyone ate together, and no one had any personal space. Some recruits took to it better than others, though it all boiled down to knowing where you sat in the pecking order.

He settled into his cot, pummelled his pillow, and pulled the itchy blankets up. There were seventy tiles on the ceiling, and he counted them every night: seven rows and ten columns of one-foot square pieces.

There was once a time when he didn't examine ceilings closely, but those memories were long gone.

That was before, and this was after.

Sudden darkness surprised him, and he checked his watch, the green glow confirming it was ten o'clock. Lights Out.

Nothing else to do but rest.

His bones ached as he sought a comfortable position, the "amazing" new mattress already developing lumps. Every night, Mick eased his form into the moulded shape before he slept. As the darkened room closed around him, exhaustion delivered him into Morpheus' arms.

***

The bus was still damp from last night and reeked of disinfectant. Mick opened the doors, allowing the early morning breeze to dissipate the stagnant air. Today's target list was long, as usual. How they expected such a small team to collect so many retrievals baffled him. The continual sorties were exhausting, and the work, although vital, was difficult on so many levels.

His group approached, their rowdy banter piercing the dawn silence. They all had work to do, and he trusted that each of the lads was capable of completing their tasks. How they woke so full of life mystified him, considering he needed at least two coffees and a punch in the face before even thinking about stepping outside.

Despite the levity suffusing the tight-knit group, discipline was never a problem. Earlier recruits had been unable to focus for long before becoming impossible to control. Unfortunately, back then, the technology was new, and the failure rate high. This latest bunch of lads took to their roles with professional ease, though. Bad days still happened, but not often. Strength in the pack, Mick reminded himself.

Everyone busied themselves with loading and checking the vehicle, leaving him to outline the day's itinerary. Geordie waited nearby, as usual, and Mick gave him a nod.

"Squad!" Geordie called. The men stood, alert.

"Thank you, Private," said Mick. He held himself ramrod straight, always starting the day with formality before everything invariably went to hell.

"We've a long list today, lads," he said. "Two confirmed contacts and three possible." The squad shuffled their feet uncomfortably. "Questions?"

"Excuse me, Corporal," said Jack. "Which sector is it today?"

"I'm afraid it's H-2 again." Mick wasn't surprised at the

collective groan. H-2 was known as Second Hell for good reason. It was a total shit show.

Every. Damn. Time.

***

The truck sat under a shady tree, the squad ready, and the SwOBR unit updated with today's calibrations. He trusted his team to do their part, but still wasn't sure the old hand-held swab reader would do its job.

The lads enjoyed their last smoke and toilet break at their favourite tree in H-2, having used this as a rendezvous point on multiple occasions. He wondered if the tree liked their company and hoped it didn't mind all the piss and cigarette butts.

Jet perched on his camp chair, his only concession towards needing a comfortable seat. The squad sat silently on the dusty ground, awaiting orders. A good unit, a fine pack of lads, all making it through basic training with high scores. Their health was tip-top, they took orders well, and other than Buddy, did not get distracted.

The Cano-Sapiens program was successful at last. Its start was rough on everyone, especially considering its high mortality rate. Mick did not fully grasp the science, but he understood that the genetic engineering improved his squad's capabilities. Human logic, in combination with enhanced canine sensory abilities, made them perfect for search and rescue.

They stood as he approached the group, splitting into their pairs—Geordie and Jack, Buddy and Alfie. He handed each their assigned coordinates and waited as they analysed them. Collectively, they turned to Jet for any last instructions.

"Eyes, ears, and snouts up today, okay?" said Jet. "Let's go."

"Well, come on," said Mick. "Move it!"

The pairs nodded at Jet, then Mick, before taking off in opposite directions. They moved quickly, and silence soon reigned over the RV point as they melted into the tall scrubland, tinderbox dry, surrounding them.

***

"Here's a brew," said Mick, passing Jet a hot metal mug. "Shouldn't be much longer." He considered the sun's position, a little past noon, while sweaty rivers ran down the small of his back, pooling at his waistband. His feet suffered similarly; his toes slippery inside his socks.

"Another warm one," said Jet. "Hope we can finish up soon."

"Yup," Mick replied.

"Don't you ever get sick of it? All this nonsense?"

"Nah, not really. Someone has to do it."

"Do they, though? You ever ask yourself what we're doing?"

"We're helping people, Jet. Simple as that."

Jet laughed, taking a swig of his tea before his expression grew dark. "No, we're not," he said quietly.

"What do you mean?"

"There's no vaccination program, mate. All lies."

"Oh, very funny. Pulling my leg, are you, old boy?"

"No."

Mick noticed a tear splash into Jet's mug. He felt as though Jet was suddenly very far away, spinning out of his reach.

"What is it? What's happened?" he asked. "I don't understand."

Jet leant forward, his eyes on the dust. When he looked up again, despair and helplessness lay in his gaze. Mick put a hand on his shoulder, offering comfort, but Jet shrugged it off, standing abruptly. "Probably nothing, just a bad night's sleep, Micky-boy."

In the distance, a whistle shrilled, putting paid to any more conversation. "The lads," said Mick. "Sounds like they have a result."

Jet smiled weakly and began to move. Both men had work to do. The quicker they did it, the better.

***

Geordie found Mick at the front of the bus. "We're ready to swab now, Boss.".

"Thanks. I'm coming," said Mick, pulling the rest of his kit from the central utility box, and switched on the unit, hoping it would start. The indicator lights flicked on; the signal looking strong. Smiling, he pulled on his gloves, put on his mask, and lowered the visor. Something was going right for a change.

The squad had assembled in the shade of the tree, a woman standing in their midst, her head covered in a rigid, vinyl hood. Muffled shouts reached Mick as he checked her vital signs. All was well.

Mick removed a swab from his kit, approaching the access point near her mouth. "Hold her steady, lads. Be gentle as you can."

He opened the valve, the negative pressure hissing as he did so. Inserting the swab, he collected a sample from inside the woman's cheek. He withdrew it carefully, placing it into the sealed SwOBR unit. Done, he released the mandibular clamp at the side of the hood, no longer needing to keep her from moving her jaw. The monitor detected an increase in heart rate—nothing of concern.

Of real concern were the rising HLA markers displayed by the SwOBR. If they showed six and above, infection was present, requiring immediate transfer to base.

The display flickered at four, then five. Mick held his breath. *Please let this bloody thing work*, he thought. The display remained at five. His shoulders fell in disappointment. He looked across at the woman, still wearing the protective hood, just as a beep drew him back to the unit. Seven.

"Shit!" said Mick.

He waved Geordie over. "A strong positive. Precautions, please."

The group bagged the woman's hands and feet before covering her in a full-length plastic gown, so long on her it dragged on the ground. Quickly, they secured her within the transport capsule at the rear of the vehicle.

Piling back on the bus, the lads gulped noisily at their water as Jet jumped into the driver's seat. Mick felt surprised but grateful for some time away from the wheel, relaxing as they pulled away. A couple of hours snoozing, and they would be home.

After a while, Jet spoke. "They're not getting vaccinated. They're getting harvested, Mick."

Mick blinked away any thought of relaxation. "What?".

"I found out by accident last night. I wish I hadn't."

"Found out what?"

"The infection isn't real, nor the vaccines. We are checking bone marrow types - HLA markers."

"No, that's not right, mate. They have the jab, then they go home."

"Have you ever seen one go home?"

"No, that's Discharge Unit's job."

"Ask the girl," said Jet, stopping the bus. "Ask her."

"How?"

"Take off her hood and ask her who's come back."

"But she's infected!"

"And you're vaccinated."

"Yes, but, I..."

"So, you can't catch it, you're safe."

Mick considered Jet's proposal. This was a man he would trust with his life. He undid his seatbelt. "Ok, then.".

Approaching the capsule, he heard weeping. He released the door lock and removed the woman's hood, revealing a girl with a pale, tear-stained face, her features contorted in terror.

"Don't kill me," she sobbed. "Please!"

"I'm not going to kill you. What's your name?".

Her only answer was the chattering of teeth, a hellish percussion reflecting her fear. Gently he said, "I'm not going to hurt you. Let's just start with your name, shall we?"

" G-Gem— Gemini."

"Are you vaccinated, Gemini? Do you understand what's happening here?"

Gemini nodded, sobbing. "You're taking me for harvest."

"No. You're getting vaccinated, sweetheart. After that, you're going home."

"No one goes home. My sister, Mila, you stole her two years ago. She hasn't come home."

"Well, I..."

"My uncle didn't come home. My friend Paul isn't home." Her voice rose till she was screaming at him. "Don't you understand? NOBODY FUCKING EVER COMES HOME!"

She began to wail. It was a primal sound, hitting Mick like a rock to the face.

He staggered backwards, expression loose with shock.

"Get out," he said, turning away. "Get out before I change my mind."

Gemini leapt from the capsule, ripping away her plastic coverings as she skittered off into the brush.

The lads' bayed from inside, excited at the idea of a second chase, bashing against the rear doors, and whooping loudly. They only settled when Mick shouted for quiet.

He climbed back into the passenger seat, keeping his eyes forward, staring unfocused into the middle distance. Trying not to look into his old friend's weary expression.

"The disease, the rescues, the vaccines?" Mick asked.

"All lies. We collect them to order; their bone marrow is sold. Nobody survives the harvesting process. We're just delivering to an abattoir."

"Fuck!" Mick shook his head. "I can't live with this. I can't."

Jet rummaged in the supply chest. "I know," he said, climbing into the back. "Nor can I."

Mick slumped against his seat, broken. Splintered thoughts pierced his mind and slashed at his heart.

THUNK-A-THUNK! THUNK!

The sudden sound made him jump.

Turning, he realised Jet had neatly put down all four lads.

"Sorry Micky-boy," he said. "We trained them for one thing and one thing only. It's not their fault. I had to stop it."

Climbing back into his seat, he offered Mick the nail gun. "Do you want to do it, or shall I?"

"Jet, my brother, do what you need to do."

Mick turned his head, gazing upwards.

No ceiling tiles to count, but he didn't mind. Soon, he would be moving to new quarters. He hoped the blankets were better.

The cold steel touched his temple. "Goodbye, old friend," said Jet. "Rest easy."

Lights out.

Effie's Eye

Effie tried again to close her left eye. Willing the lid to roll over her eyeball. She tried to supply some protection against the icy assault. The soft, pink flesh refused to budge. She had no feeling in her face, let alone her eye. She had long since stopped producing any tears that would warm or lubricate the surface. Effie owned this frozen eye, forever open.

Beneath the conjunctiva, the muscles of the iris dilated and constricted. Effie was able to notice movement and change in the light but unable to make out forms. Her head held in a fixed position, forwards facing into the violence and wind.

A pilots' mask clamped to her face, limpet-like, supplying breathable air. She thought she may have been here for hours. A windy glacier dragged itself across her skin. The slow destruction causing her jaws to grind, intent on destroying their own teeth.

If not for the burning agony in her eye, she may have been circumspect as to the events leading up to this predicament. She may have reconsidered some of her decisions and chosen a different course of action. Effie had already realised it was too late for regrets.

What she said is what she had said. She would take

everything back in an instant if it meant she might shut her eye. All she wanted was the window seat in order to watch the world speeding away behind her. Should she have acquiesced to the old lady straight away?

Perhaps.

In fact, now she knew better; most definitely.

The temperature tumbled and the wind shear increased, the skin around her socket ripped away from her cheek. It was as if the wind caught a gap in the outside corner and made use of that to pry the epidermis from the underlying structure. Similar to a piece of packing tape being slowly pulled apart. There wasn't any pain, just a cold, tugging sensation. A beige blur hurtled into her eye and flew away behind her.

The newly exposed nerve endings joined in with the discordance Effie suffered. A fire burnt in her face, sharpened forks tested the meat for tenderness. Yet still the cold, the bone-brittle cold, lashed her open eye. The air rushed into her face. The mask stopped her from losing her breath, but her eye would not endure much more.

Gradually, the tissues containing the vitreous humour of the eyeball rent themselves asunder, which allowed viscous fluid to slide away into the wind.

The last thing Effie experienced was the slippery discharge blowing backwards into her freezing ear. Then all became ever-dark and silent.

***

In seat B-54, Ms. Felicity Harland sipped at her gin and tonic. The service on this journey had been first class, though her ticket said "Standard". She decided she would write to the train company this afternoon to commend them on their excellent staff.

The steward who removed the rude young woman had been an absolute gentleman. He understood these young people needed to be shown that the virtue of their youth does not entitle them to take what they want.

He had frog-marched the girl and her bags into the corridor and away to the guard's carriage. He'd winked at Felicity and said, "Don't worry, she'll get to have a window all to herself until Euston."

Always comforting to know some people continued to keep an eye out for the older generation, thought Felicity.

It was like a breath of fresh air.

101 Words

I've built a fence around these words. They seem settled now. Earlier, they made a bid for freedom by jumping off the page. I coaxed them back with the promise of tea and Oxford commas.

In the far corner, I am sure singing has begun. I can see a carousel and a hoopla stall. Most of the words seem happy.

The adverbs are hanging around the verbs' toilets, but I presume that's normal. The other verbs are in one spot just *doing* things, as usual.

The proper nouns aren't speaking to anyone uncapitalised.

I can't even begin to describe the adjectives!

Rainy Day - Easy Prey.

There it was again; the "Sniff and the Skip" as she called it. The noise they made once they had committed to the chase. At her back, the soft tread of rubber soles on the rainy pavement confirmed her judgement. She could almost feel the excitement rising in the presence behind her as she picked her way through the puddles, trying not to slip or trip. Not wanting to appear vulnerable as she tried to get home.

She clutched her bag tight to her chest, the soft leather moulded into her coat, she almost buttoned it inside to stop what came next. Wanting to make it disappear, to make it invisible.

Nothing to see here, leave me alone.

Without warning, one of the long straps slithered, serpent-like, under her arm and dangled tantalisingly at her side. She shuddered as she realised she had rung the dinner bell for the vulpine follower.

This was the part she detested most, the dance of predator and prey. It sickened her to her long bones how the weak fell afoul of the ravenous. Why the hunger? Why the need to feed on others? This was exhausting; all she wanted was the quiet enjoyment of a walk and some fresh Autumn air. Now, here she was again, back amongst the hunt.

Behind her, the cough drew her attention back to the moment. She tucked her bag tighter in against her body, it was becoming difficult to conceal as she concentrated on increasing her pace. The pale light was leeching away into the October night, the trees shadowy onlookers, rubbing their creaky boughs together in anticipation of a kill after dusk.

Another ten minutes and it would be dark, she reasoned. The streetlight which sometimes supplied a pool of well-lit sanctuary on this deserted corner was still broken and useless. The bloody council had done nothing as usual.

She hurried to turn right into the next road, she wasn't running yet. Knowing if she ran, it would only make the end more violent. She reached the corner and from the side of her eye glimpsed a slim built man, nondescript; his sport shoes reflecting the light, giving his feet the appearance of hovering above the ground.

She spun around the wall, using her right hand to help her turn the ninety degrees. Her bag slipped down, still on her shoulder but no longer tight against her. It rolled and writhed as she tried to catch hold again, her hands sliding on the soft leather which came alive in her hands.

The sickening feeling of dread returned.

The prey. She did not think she could survive this ordeal again.

She hated this, hated the hunt. Cursed the predator, spat her anger into the night; her breath in small, staccato vapour clouds left her body. She stumbled and slid to the floor. Grabbing at the bag, she spun around to see the boy (because he was a boy) reach her in two strides. His face opened in a grin, exposing broken teeth and a wedge of gum in his cheek.

He leaned down closer to her, she caught the bitter reek of cheap cider and tobacco oozing from him. He reached out towards her. For one second, she thought he might help her up. Unabashed, he grabbed at the bag clutched to her chest. She understood that the hunt was at its climax. To the victor the spoils and so forth.

She let go, untangling her hands from the straps and allowing the clasp to fall open as she noticed his eyes glistening with the thrill of the chase and the prospect of reward. The eternal chasing down of the vulnerable.

It would never change whilst the predator had hunger and the prey had weaknesses. His eyes never left hers as he reached inside the bag, rummaging in her things, her private things, her secret things.

An expression of disappointment flickered across his face, and he cast her an angry glance. He opened the jaws of the bag wider and peered inside, angling the opening to catch what little light there was. Spying something of interest, he reached in up to his elbow and grinned as he appeared to have found something to hold on to. The bag writhed and trembled, taking a breath.

The boy's eyes grew to inky dark saucers, his mouth formed a circle, as though about to blow a smoke ring. He didn't make a sound other than to gasp as he twitched and jerked. The only sounds were the soft, wet crushing and snorting noises from inside the bag. Inch by excruciating inch, more of the boy disappeared into the leathery mouth. The reflective strips on his feet danced with each jerky movement, as it sucked the bone marrow and liquor out of his dry shell.

She knew it would soon be over. Remembering the hunt always ended with a feast, her thoughts turned to her own repast. She wondered if she had enough cheese in the fridge for a sandwich when she got home. She couldn't face another trek to the High Street. This was the third time she had been out this afternoon, and she hadn't yet got as far as the corner shop. She cursed herself for not having taken anything out of the freezer this morning. She may have to phone for a take-away instead.

The noises faded now, less slobbering, and more dusty puffing. The bag became still, the clasp closed with a crisp click, its breathing once again undetectable. She pushed herself up from the damp concrete and reached back down for the bag.

There came the faint grinding of tooth on bone and the gentle scampering of unspeakable paws from deep inside the receptacle. She slung the wriggling bag over her shoulder, knocked the dirty leaves from her coat, and stood tall once more.

She was sure she had enough cheese, no need to waste money on a takeaway. Maybe she would head out tomorrow and treat herself to a pub lunch. This sounded like a better plan.

"Yes," she said.

She tiptoed over the bloodied, discarded trainers and turned towards home.

Poetry Snacks

Last touch

    When I'm dying, don't bring me flowers or prophets.
    Don't whisper as if there is shame in death.
    Put me by the window.
    let sunlight play in my hair.
    Read to me, teach me something new. Sing.
    When I am dying, don't bring me flowers or prophets.
Bring me you.

Pictures of Dad

    I have no picture
    In which I stand next to you.
    I held on to
    The camera, never your hand.
    No proof that
    You knew me, though
    I came from you.
    The pixels reflect
    Only the light - Not your love.

Cenotaph

You charge me not to forget
when you failed to remember
as the rattling of sabres
delivered you to Hell's kiss.

I'm asked to respect
those now gone forever
who followed the drumbeat
into the Abyss.

And I look at the faces
of those who had fallen
as their mates bore them
home upon their shoulders,

from the black and white moments
kept by those who adored them
their youth smiles back
as we grow older.

How can I forgo
the lessons you learnt
for me and my children
as you fought to be free?

Now why is it that I
watch my son hear the drummer
straight up his head
and follow your lead?

The day comes soon
when I, somebody's grieving mother,
will wring my hands
and rend my breast,

then your words will fall
on bomb-blast ears,
that lie,
"Dulce et Decorum Est."

The Slips

Don't say anything.

Lay where you are.

Don't move. We haven't got long; a minute or two, so close that mouth and open those ears.

I'm here, underneath you.

No. No, don't jump out of bed. Stay still, don't start shouting, either.

I'm under the bed.

I always have been. Well, since you were five, at least. Remember when you first started dreaming about monsters? Remember when you heard breathing and felt something grab at you as you leapt into bed? Yeah, well that was about the time I showed up. I have been here ever since.

Stop it. Stop it! Stop sobbing, you're wasting time.

Stop.

STOP.

OK, just breathe.

Breathe, breathe; nice and easy. I'm going to explain all this to you again, for the umpteenth time. I wish you would stop forgetting, but this is the way things are for us. Part of the bloody job, I suppose.

All is OK. You'll be OK, please try to stop shaking. You're rattling the headboard. Breathe in and out really slowly. OK?

Are we good?

Sure?

Here we go. Before I start, please try not to shriek this time. It's not helpful and no-one is coming to save you. No-one ever came before, and they are not going to now. So, don't bother.

I'm serious. Don't.

Are you ready? Wave your hand down here if you are.

Hey! Wave your hand, I said, not jab me in the face. I'm already uncomfortable enough, trying to fit under here every night. Not to mention when you are not alone and there are two of you up above and two of us underneath. It's bloody restrictive, and not at all conducive to a peaceful night.

Thankfully, you're not in some threesome. I've read that it's almost impossible to fit three in, and we don't qualify for an exemption from duty due to sexual activity. We only receive a pass if the number of participants is over five. Five? The atmosphere would be like a bloody mosh pit down here.

The smell? Not great. Not great at all.

Sorry. Didn't mean to ramble. OK, this is the rundown, listen in and stay calm.

Calm, OK?

I am one of The Slips. There are about as many of us Slips as there are humans over five. Psychopaths and the dying don't have The Slips. They get Thuds and The Crowd respectively. Too much to go into now, but suffice to say, most humans get The Slips.

Before you are old enough to need The Slips, you are assigned Lights. They are much more pleasant, don't live under the bed, and remain visible until proper speech begins, and then they become "imaginary friends" for a while.

This is when we arrive; The Slips, that is. Every night, under your bed. I'll remain until you need The Crowd. Most importantly, I will be here when The Weight comes. The Weight is coming, I can sense it. You'll start to feel it soon, too.

The Weight comes to feed. On you.

Sorry if that's blunt, but the truth is the truth. The Weight will hold you down, tight as a drum skin over the bed. Sleep paralysis? All those theories? Utter nonsense. It's The Weight feeding, the dirty thing. The Weight will drain out some, but not all, of your soul-sap.

It hurts a bit, so I'm told, but The Weight promised us they won't dry you up like an empty corn husk. Sometimes they become greedy and come close to sucking all parts of You out, in which case us Slips step to one side for The Crowd. That shouldn't happen tonight. Don't worry.

And if that does happen, you'll recognise someone in The Crowd, I'm sure.

You should go with them, it'll be fine.

Wait.

I feel it, I do. It's here. The Weight.

Don't be scared. If you scream, it gets excited and can't stop its filthy feeding.

Try not to be frightened, it's going to crawl over here and jump up on the bed.

You'll feel the paws land and hear the head slithering behind. Make sure you don't look and don't be afraid. Try to relax.

It's here. You'll forget this by the morning, one way or another.

Just breathe.
Here it comes. One little hop.

There.

Sleep tight, my little one.

The Unbearable Weight of Truth

The words which we don't dare to speak,
are the words that weigh us down.
The silent words that tell of pain,
are those that help us drown.

The stories that we cannot tell
are those that keep us bound.
The things that we can never say,
will hold us underground.

The truths that can't be said aloud,
are those that stop our breath.
The sentences that set us free,
unspoken, hasten death.

The darkness that we keep close by,
in the suffocating still.
The nothing we believe we are,
the void we never fill.

Though in the gloom; a spark, a breeze
of something simply kind.
A hand that reaches in the fire,
bids us leave it all behind.

To tell our truth, to damn those lies,
is to walk in light unknown.
The freedom that we yearn for now,
grows the seed that hope has sown.

Her Solitude

"The deep-recessed vision—all was blight;
Lamia, no longer fair, there sat a deadly white"

Another pebble hit the window and bounced away, doing no damage. The sound of small feet receding down the alleyway followed; some catcalls floating up on the wind, but nothing definable. Another Saturday morning, the usual time for stones and shouting. But maybe fewer rotten leaves stuffed through the letterbox, seeing as it wasn't quite spring yet, but that didn't preclude the possibility of twigs or dog muck. The substances, though, relied on the creativity, or perhaps ingenuity, of the kids involved.

Little sods, Lamia thought, wondering if their parents knew, or cared, what they got up to when they played in the street. The long, silent days of lockdown had proved a blessing, no children around for weeks on end. Truthfully, she did not understand the issue with kids sitting indoors, adrift in computer games and social media. The more they stayed away from her home, the happier she was.

***

"I hope you love the place, Ms. Lammy," said the rental agent at the viewing. "An abundance of trees, shops, and families make for a pleasant community."

"Quite," came Lamia's reply, not convinced but keen for a change of habitat.

In reality, this was a mediocre area, with neighbours who kept to themselves. However, it didn't take the local children long to discover her and begin the harassment she experienced wherever she made her home.

***

So, as per normal on a Saturday, she found herself at the kitchen window, considering her view of the park and its playground equipment. The brightly coloured installations remained damp from an earlier drizzle, swings moving listlessly as the local starlings squabbled over perching rights.

Lamia did not care to be part of the world. Windows existed only as annoying holes in perfectly adequate walls. Perhaps she would brick them over, reverting to something akin to cave-dwelling. A chuckle slipped out as she imagined the neighbourhood troublemakers flicking pebbles at the concrete, having no detrimental effect on her shelter at all.

She adjusted her glasses, thick lenses with new and expensive coatings. They enabled her to view the bird life in the trees opposite with greater clarity. If she wanted to read, however, she swapped spectacles and turned on a bright light. Books were her refuge, the rocks she clung to in the roiling waters which swamped her dreadful life.

The weekly drop-off was due in a few hours. She hoped the package would arrive promptly today. Last week had been an unmitigated disaster. The misdirected delivery was irretrievable and not easily replaced. A miserable weekend ensued, not improving until they sent a substitute on Monday. She loathed the fact she depended on others for her well-being.

With a jolt, she remembered she needed to rinse and return her recyclables and quickly found the small, empty jars. All bore an icon of a baby with a spoon. The brand had not changed its logo for over eighty years, the image instantly recognisable to loyal subscribers. She gave each jar a scrub with soapy water, rinsed off the suds and let the liquid drain away into the sink.

***

The clean glassware clinked in its holder as she padded down the hallway towards her front door. It opened for a second; she checked both ways along her alley and placed the empties on the step for this afternoon's collection. The door locked once more, she returned to her kitchen.

The appetite inside awoke and sleepily stretched itself. Saturdays were always the worst day for her. These final few hours of waiting hurt the most. The effects of last night's supplements waned. The growls in her stomach raised angry voices. Glad she kept nothing in the house which would satisfy this craving, she allowed herself a calming breath. She had invested too much time and too many tears to throw everything away in a moment of weakness.

Distraction usually helped her to push through the empty minutes on days like these. She went through to her sparsely furnished lounge. On the coffee table, she found her favourite book. Making herself comfortable in her tattered armchair, she sighed and opened the volume at her bookmark.

She had found sanctuary in Thomas Bewick's "A History of British Birds" for many years. The exquisite wood-engravings of the various species gave her a sense of calm. Lamia would often recite the names and classifications aloud. The sound of the ancient words soothed her.

Today, she intended to enjoy one of her favourites, The Great Bustard. The illustration was particularly detailed, each feather delicately traced on its wing. Her thin finger ran over the picture as she followed every line. Satisfied, she sighed with pleasure. What a magnificent creature. As per Bewick, the bird also proved quite tasty when roasted.

Her gut growled again. She squinted at the clock. It was already noon. Her restlessness grew. Lamia returned to her book. Perhaps there was some distraction in the yellowed pages. Her attention drawn to a rather handsome "Musk Duck", she started to study its description.

Crack! A stone struck her window with some force. She took a deep breath and continued to read. Her intestine, now a piece of ragged cloth, turned inside out with hunger.

Ping! There it was again. This time, she caught the sounds of laughter and footsteps as they approached the front door.

"Please go away," Lamia said in a tiny voice. An icy tear appeared on her cheek and tracked down toward her chin. "Please."

The letterbox gave a metallic snap, followed by a wet thud. Lamia stood, peering down the hallway. On the mat lay a half-eaten hamburger. She could not help but catch the scent of the meat and salivated involuntarily.

From the other side of the door, the giggles and whispers intensified. The slot opened again, a small hand poked through and deposited yet more rubbish. Dirt and tissue paper tumbled down to the floor. The culprit's sleeve snagged on the way out, and they needed to wriggle to extricate themselves.

Lamia sniffed, suckling at the air briefly puffing through the small space. Something roused her appetite. Yearning brushed cold fingers over her skin.

She moved closer to the door. The rattle came again. The hand was having some difficulty fitting the next object through successfully.

She tilted her head, watching, listening, inhaling, tasting. Her lips drew back. She ran her tongue across them. Drool leeched from her jowls, hanging from her maw in long silver ribbons. She latched on to the scent of the food. She snuffled at the door.

The hand wriggled, finally squeezing the fingers, the palm, and a dead rat through the gap.

The hunger won. Lamia leapt forward, mouth open, teeth bared, ready to feed.

She bit down, clamped her muscular jaws shut with a sickening crunch. She crushed the tender young bones, swallowed the hand whole, including the rodent in its clutch. A howl and a terror-filled wail assaulted the silence. Other feet took shrieking flight, the noise echoed in retreat along the alley.

Lamia flung the door asunder and stared down into the tar-like eyes of a pale brown-haired boy. He screamed and clutched at the stump of his right arm, his young blood coming in short, intense spurts. Vermilion droplets flew up into her face, a sprinkling of coppery rain.

Lamia, her thirst raging, licked the warm blood from her lips. She put her mouth to the fountain and fed. Tearful smears mingled with congealing claret spatters on his blanching face as Lamia sucked the juice from the shell of the child.

She rocked back on to her haunches, her tongue chasing every small glob of the iron-rich nutrients now sticky on her limbs. The satisfaction was short-lived for the daemon, it was time for her to move on once more. She would be gone at sunset, there was too much to explain away this time.

***

Nobody noticed the opaque woman who made her way across the park, a heavy book tucked under her arm. Looking neither left nor right, she dissolved into the filthy dark. And thus, she returned to the eternal torment of her crushing solitude.

Crossing on a burnt bridge

Brandon Harvey reeked of despair and last night's booze. The former "Rising Star of Greenstreet Investments" had cremated his laurels along with his burgeoning career. His future not so much bleak as absent, due to his taking the wrong fork in the road of life.

He turned sideways to the cell wall, pressing his face into the cool surface. *Why was he so stupid?* A scream burnt in his chest. *You bloody fool! You ridiculous, bloody fool!* He took a shuddering breath, closing his eyes. The concrete remained cold, anchoring him to his presence. He exhaled, the air fluttering through his pursed lips.

On another bench, a pile of filthy clothes moved. A ferret-like figure appeared. A man held together by layers of clothing, topped off with a greasy woollen hat. Everything he wore appeared to be not quite the rational side of brown.

Brandon did not wish to talk to this unfortunate creature. He was suffering enough without being drawn into some drunkard's drama.

"Did ya? Did ya do it?" said the man.

"I don't want to talk about it," Brandon replied, sitting up and leaning forward to stare at the floor.

"Did ya, though? Do the bad thing? The mad thing?"

"That is none of your business."

"Like it, did ya?" The man stumbled to his feet, lurching towards Brandon. "Wanna do it again?"

He remembered once smelling spoiled meat. This was worse, much worse. He pushed himself back into the wall.

"Did ya kill her? Dead?"

Brandon shouted as he stood. "Get away from me!"

"Did ya? Tell ol' Nicky. I can help."

Dread joined the conversation, along with anguish and damnation. Soft black snowflakes hummed around the small space.

"Don't mind them flies. Better tell ol' Nicky what ya did."

The last of Brandon's logical thought slithered away. He whispered, "I was only showing off."

With a gaping grin, Nicky said, "Did ya drink? Take a drive? Did ya hit the girl?"

Brandon's sobs punctuated the silence.

"Did ya drag her? Dying? Dump her like a dog into a ditch?"

Shoulders heaving, he nodded. Nicky patted him with a dirty hand.

"I'll help ya, boy. Sign here. For your soul, like." Nicky produced a cigarette packet and a pencil. Brandon wrote his name across the logo.

"What will you do?" he asked.

"I'll fix this, boy. You're mine, now." Nicky winked.

He'd forged a deal with The Devil. Was it possible he could have everything back again? Perhaps there was still hope.

The cell door opened. An officer entered, handcuffs ready.

"Harvey? Come with me, we're charging you with murder."

"Hey! No! He made a deal with me!" Brandon pointed at Nicky.

"Again? What'd I tell you last week, Nicholas?" the officer said. "You gotta take your pills every day. Stop lying to these folks. Crazy old bastard."

He chuckled, nodding at Brandon who grudgingly stepped forward to be cuffed.

His rising star now in free fall, Brandon shuffled through the door into a desolate future with not a single laurel in his sight.

Chairs to be stacked away, please.

There was a small, raised platform at the far end of the hall. Upon it sat an upright piano. The tiny stage had an unfortunate slope which leant towards the meagre footlights. A low guard-rail had been installed to prevent performers sliding into the audience.

The hall itself smelt of toddlers and jumble sales. The scars on the wooden flooring told of high heels and over eager miniature-railway enthusiasts. A red fire bucket hung precariously on one wall, a long-handled window hook leaning against it.

In the centre of the room, someone had set up a small circle of plastic chairs. In the middle of the circle was a low table, upon which was a box of tissues, some paper, and a variety of pens. This central part was well lit, the edges of the space darkened like a vignette.

At the back of the hall, a door opened, protesting with a creaking groan. Warm air accompanied the first attendee, the interior being cooler than the outside. As the person stepped towards the central lighting, their shape became clearer. A man, resplendent in a neon blue body suit, walked to the chair the furthest away from the door. Stretching the material around his groin and upper thighs to allow for movement, he sat and adjusted himself accordingly.

Next to arrive were two women, one looked middle-aged, the other appeared older and frailer. They nodded at the blue man and took their seats to his immediate left. As they sat, a tanned, muscular man strode into the room. He was symmetrical and good-looking in a vacuous kind of way. He winked at the women, ignoring the man in blue. He sat at nine o'clock, pulled out his phone, and became seemingly oblivious to everything else.

The remaining seats filled over the next few minutes. There was a poorly dressed, bearded man who came in, sniffing and clearing his throat. He sat next to Mr Perfect, which caused him to shuffle uncomfortably. Also in the group was a Druid, a barista, a Cross-Channel swimmer, a large man with "Security" written on his black jacket, and a dishevelled woman in a dressing-gown. Each seat occupied. The atmosphere became tense.

"Thank you all for coming," said the dishevelled woman. "I have called this meeting to help us refocus."

The group exchanged nervous glances, except for the Druid, busy trying to retrieve a sparrow out of his hat.

"I know we were in the midst of a bumpy few months, but we got through it in the end," the woman continued. "I'm grateful for that."

"Look," said Blue. "I want to know when I can change out of this bloody thing." He snapped his Lycra sleeves loudly against his skin.

"Well, sorry to say, you chose that outfit. Choose something else if you want to change."

"No, that's your job." said Blue "This outfit has been stuck like this for ages."

"I want to do something else; I am sick of coffee-idiots." said the barista.

"You were supposed to be a florist, Larry!" said the woman. "You picked bloody Cafe Soy-Soy, not me!"

"I thought it would make me more interesting," said Larry with a pout. "It only made me cross."

"Right," said the woman. "Who else isn't happy in their current role?"

Everybody raised their hands except Mr Perfect and the Druid. One was on the phone and the other had wandered off to examine the content of the fire bucket.

The woman turned to the swimmer. "What's your problem?"

"I'm f-f-freezing! It's w-w-winter and I've r-r-run out of g-g-goose f-f-fat." he shivered, teeth all jittery-chattery.

"I told you to go into competitive vegetable growing. But, oh no! You wanted more recognition. Well, this is what you got." The woman shook her head in despair.

She turned to the two friends. "What about you, two? Are you unhappy, as well?"

"Oh no, dear, I think we're doing alright. What do you think, Bess?" said the older woman to her companion.

"We're fine, thanks," said Bess. "Ivy and I are having a smashing time. Quite exciting, really."

"Why did you both put your hands up then?"

"Oh, sorry. We thought you said something about rolls, and we're both a bit peckish."

"Good grief. I give up!" she checked around the circle to see who she had missed.

"I put my hand up because I don't enjoy doing this security malarkey," grumbled Security Man. "I wanted a gun, not a torch."

"I made it quite clear that there were to be no guns. You only chose security because you hoped for a Taser at the very least. Quite frankly, I'm thinking of having you killed."

"What? Why?"

"Because I'm tired of you and your ilk. You are one-dimensional and stereotypical. I don't think I need you anymore."

Security man gulped. "I can do better," he whispered. "I like dogs and I sponsor a goat in Wyoming."

The woman narrowed her eyes at him. "I'll think about it."

"Mr Sniffer, how are you travelling?"

"Piss off."

"Great. Thanks for that. Put your hand up just to swear at me? Marvellous."

"Kiss me arse!"

"OK, moving on.... Sexy boy. How's it hanging?"

Mr Perfect glanced up from his phone and flashed a smouldering grin. Long dormant uteri roused themselves from their slumber. Ovaries within a twenty-mile radius burst into life. In the distance, sirens could be heard.

"Crikey, I can see why I don't use you very often. Dial it back, Sexy. You can't afford the child support."

She swept her eyes round the room, finally catching sight of the Druid. He was arranging some spider webs into magical patterns. Oblivious to his surroundings, he giggled and chanted as he worked.

"I thought you would do okay, my dear friend. You just needed to be set free." The woman smiled and sat back in her seat, appearing relaxed for the first time.

"Righto, guys," she said. "We'll have another crack at this. Please try to stay in the character that I write for you."

"But..." said Security.

"No buts, we have to make this work. I need to finish this bloody book."

"Will there be any refreshments?" asked Ivy.

"Ooh, good question," said Bess.

The woman sighed. "Look, if we can reach the end of this first draft, I promise we can have a nice tea together. How does that sound?"

"What about coffee? The proper stuff with caffeine and everything?" asked Larry.

"Oh, we will definitely need caffeine, my friend."

Larry smiled, tucking his white tea-towel into his belt.

"So, in summary; we are all going to stay in our characters. No one is going to go rogue and change the whole bloody plot because they had 'an idea'. Is that clear?"

Nods all round; except, of course, from the Druid who was thinking about photosynthesis.

"Fantastic! Meeting over. Now let me go back to sleep." The woman rolled over and found the cool side of the pillow.

They stacked the chairs as per hall hire policy and drifted away.

Last to leave was the Druid who, with a wink that popped out of the page, turned off the lights and closed the door behind him.

A note from the author.

Thank you for reading this far.

I hope you found something in this lucky dip that amused or engaged you.

I am planning to publish my first full length novel in 2023 (pandemics and alien invasions notwithstanding). On the next couple of pages is a little teaser of what may or may not be in the works.

At the back of the book, you will also find some useful and worthy links to people that I admire; some of whom have helped me in my writing journey.

As for you, dear reader, I'd love to hear from you, unless you want to tell me to take up stamp collecting instead of writing. In which case, you can go butter a crumpet with your eyes shut, as far as I am concerned.

This work (of whatever it is) has been mainly completed with one cat asleep on the printer and two dogs snoring underneath my desk. Buster, our elder cat, has aided me with editing and promotion. The other three animals have been utterly useless.

Made Away Themselves

By Rachel K Jones
Coming in 2023

Get ready for a tale that has been festering in a small Essex town for over four-hundred years.
There will be a lot of tea and possibly some Bingo.

How exciting!

Prologue

The air disappeared from the room, ripping itself from Donna's lungs. She gutted and gasped. Her mouth yapping and yawing as she drowned in the brightly lit space. He had taken all the oxygen with him. His last act was to condemn her to an excruciating suffocation.

The vacuum she now inhabited sucked her soul through her chest. No resistance came from her ribs. They gave in to the stronger force.

She watched as he became a decreasing smudge in the dim hallway. Surrounded, as usual, by those who worshiped him and his "tremendous courage". They were all liars and thieves. They pretended it was "his considered decision to leave, nothing personal, a hard thought-out choice" when it was time to move on.

She knew a lie when she heard one. She recognised a coward's exit when she saw one. Donna also realised the whole of their relationship was so meaningless to him he could just leave when he felt it was time to go.

The bastard.

The lying, shitting bastard.

All those promises which slipped out of his lips, sliding

down his oily chin. A salad of false hopes. A fucking breakfast buffet of platitudes. Now she choked on the leftovers. Fighting for air in this fetid pressure-cooker of a room.

Blood dripped into her lap from the gouges in her palms. Her nails had shredded her hands in her fury at his betrayal. She had the Stigmata of the Lost.

Maybe the wounds would never heal. Maybe she should keep opening the cuts with scissors whenever she thought of the mockery of the time they had together.

He was a fucking liar. She was left to deal with the monumental parcel of shit that was the fallout. She had to face the wrath of those whom he had hurt.

For God's sake, she had to talk to the bloody police. This was the extent of his betrayal, his final middle finger for her to swivel on. Liar, cruel coward, thief, and tormentor.

Finally, she sucked in a lungful of stale air. The room stank of him and his shit. The filthy, pathetic bastard.

She didn't know how she was going to live without him.

Chapter One

Donna gazed around the room. There were perhaps thirty people here; both young and old, silently waiting with slumped shoulders which spoke of bone-weariness. The walls papered with long-faded fragments of information, direction, judgement, and remonstration. It appeared every waiting person was being cross-examined, their fate wavering in the balance. Each seat's occupant had the same haggard look of the long-guilty who expects to receive a heavy penalty.

Those who could, contorted themselves into positions of less discomfort; shuffling feet, crossing legs, and trying to shift their weight from one hip to another. In the corner by the door, a small boy snuffled and tried to burrow into his mother's arms. The mother, red-eyed, noticed the disproving frowns and quietly shushed her child. An old man coughed, causing the crowd to turn towards him with angry stares.

Donna could hear footsteps echoing down the long hallway and approaching the door; the crowd drew a collective breath, some even readied themselves in anticipation of what was to come. The door slid open with an electric sigh; a masked face peered into the gloom, intrusively searching each set of eyes. In silence, the people stared back.

"Mr. Groves?" called the voice behind the mask. "Jack Groves?"

The old man stood, adjusted his own mask, and coughed again. He stepped towards the figure standing at the open door. "Yes, love," he mumbled. "That's me."

"Come this way please, Mr. Groves."

The figure gestured towards the hallway and stepped back to allow the old man space to manoeuvre his frail, bowed frame through the gap. The door hissed shut behind them both. Those staying stared at the two distorted figures still visible through the frosted glass.

"Well, that ain't right!" said a woman sporting an argumentative haircut. "I was here long before that old bloke."

She stood, adjusted her face mask, and stomped towards Donna at the reception counter. Standing directly in front of her, the woman rapped on the plastic partition that separated the receptionists from the waiting room and shouted through the gap.

"Why has he gone in? I've been waiting here for two hours, and I was here well before the old man. I'm next!"

Donna checked her watch; only half-past eight, and they were already off and running. At the back of her mind, the long day cracked opened its ghastly maw, and she tumbled, helpless, into the murky depths. At the end of her shift, it would regurgitate her out on the street, freeing her to return home. Until then, she was doomed to swim in the beast's digestive chowder with the ungrateful, simpering idiots who occupied the orange vinyl chairs in front of her.

She dragged a smile across her face; it was as old and withered as the posters on the clinic walls, but no-one really cared. It was part of the choreography of passive survival; you can look like shit, but no-one will mention anything. If somebody -- anybody -- is struggling, everyone else can breathe easier.

"Miss Bentley," Donna began. "I'm sorry you feel forgotten. Your turn will be soon. As for waiting for two hours, I didn't notice you this morning when I opened the clinic. I can only presume you must have been standing outside in the dark. I'm afraid that doesn't count as waiting time."

The Bentley woman sniffed and grunted her displeasure. Unable to meet Donna's gaze, she walked, without enthusiasm, back to her seat. Donna leaned back in her chair and adjusted her phone headset.

The waiting room still seemed a little restless, but she had easily stifled the first sign of revolt and now the rest of the buggers should stay quiet for a while. It was a lot more subdued nowadays, anyway, with all patients wearing masks whilst on the premises.

Donna quite liked this new masked normality at work. It gave her a good excuse to avoid conversation and to opt out of social encounters with other staff members. A small win in a lousy year, she supposed.

Not that she detested humanity in its entirety. She just could not bear weak people, these people. The same faces that came back week after week. They were always needing someone else to fix them, never trying to fix themselves.

She remembered the tourist fish-feeding trips in Thailand. At certain times of the day, you could buy large pots of fish food with which to hand feed the marine life. It always struck Donna as being slightly tragic, that these beautiful creatures gathered every day to eat from a bucket of slops because it was an easy food source for them.

Their greedy fish mouths blew gasping bubbles as they consumed kilograms of processed crap. The tourists loved it, the tour guides made money, and the fish got fattened nicely, set to be served as the signature dish at a tropical banquet. This was the circle of life thing those cartoon lions got excited about. It came back to survival choreography. It was all utter nonsense.

Turning back to the phone lines, Donna spotted some calls on hold. On went her smile, button pushed, greetings exchanged, and round and round and round she goes. The fax machine clicked and whirred, the computers mumbled, and patients huffed whilst the reception door hissed as they called the sick and lazy through in turn.

Donna again felt the grinding of the great beast's jaws as it masticated her deeper into the day.

"Roll on, home time", she said to no-one.

No-one was listening, anyway.

***

"What do you mean, Paul?" George spat. "What kind of 'clerical error' are we talking about?"

Paul shifted in his chair and cleared his throat. "A minor accounting problem, sort of, in the primary data source."

George fixed him with a steely gaze. "Blaming the tech now, are we?"

"No, George, it's a real problem, a previously undetected fault in the GRS."

"Nonsense! That thing is bloody bulletproof. Those downstairs extensively tested it. Extensively, Paul."

Paul knew he did not have the extra minutes to waste arguing with George. Time was slipping away from him, and the project deadline loomed large. He pressed the intercom.

"Summon John for me please, Linda." he said

"Right away, sir," came the tinny reply.

George sat on the edge of the desk, gazing out of the window.

Paul pecked at his keyboard, frustration apparent.

John appeared in the doorway; an eyebrow raised in query. "Ladies," he smirked. "How can I be of help?" He flopped down into one of the leather chairs and crossed his ankle over his knee, revealing a glint of silvery silk hosiery.

"Paul says the GRS is faulty!" George exclaimed.

"No, I didn't. What I said, *George*, was that there was a fault in it. Not that the whole bloody thing was faulty." Paul sighed and rubbed his chin.

"A problem with the software, but how?" said John, leaning forward. "Can you sort it out?"

"Not without help," Paul said, pointing at his computer screen. "This is way out of my league."

"Let's get Tech up here, quick-smart to see what they advise." George said, the panic growing in his voice. "I'll get Linda to call them."

A second later, the unerring Linda walked into the room, accompanied by a young man, lost in his mobile phone. She elbowed him in the ribs to get his attention; he lowered his device and looked up at the three expectant faces in front of him.

"John, Paul, George," said Linda. "This is Dingo."

"G'day!" he said with a devilish grin. "Call me Darren if you would prefer. Whatever suits."

(To be continued...)

Contact Me

email: rainyarvo@gmail.com

blog: RachelKJones.me

twitter: @jonesywritenow

www.facebook.com/jonesyagain

Amazon author page: www.amazon.com/author/rkjones

Other stuff: linktr.ee/rachelkjones

Some kind of caffeine cult: www.buymeacoffee.com/rainyarvoA

About The Author

About the Author

Rachel K Jones lives in Katherine, Northern Territory, Australia.
She is originally from Essex, UK.
She enjoys writing, coleslaw, socks, and fruit-bats.
One day she hopes to go to space.
In the meantime she is a full-time nurse.

She lives with her husband, Steve, and a collection of furry mammals.

About the Book

I have put together a collection of my work from the last four decades.

The first piece is a poem I wrote when I was nine years old. I can still recall it word for word.

The most recent offerings have been written over the past few years.

I used a long-handled spoon to get everything from the bottom of the jar. The dregs, if you will.

All mistakes are my own. I have left a few in there to see if you are paying attention.

Enjoy the peephole into my brain.

Please wipe your feet.

Useful Stuff

- **Katherine Region of Writers** – Meet on the second Saturday of the month at Katherine Library. Details: facebook.com/KathWriters

- **The Inkwell Writing Collective** - A writing collective founded on Discord. Dedicated to supporting and helping others hone their craft and achieve publication. Twitter: @TheInkwellWC

- **RTSlaywood** – Mentor, Meme-King, Inspiration. Twitter: @RTSlaywood   Linktree: linktr.ee/RTSlaywood

- **ABlachernae** – Author of the world's most beautiful book about love. Twitter: @a_baguette_a   Linktree: linktr.ee/A.Blachernae

- **NovelPad.com** – Most intuitive writing tool I have ever used.

Notes